Contents

The Dog
and his
Reflection

Once upon a time there was a dog who
had a piece of meat. He was carrying it
home in his mouth to eat in peace. On his way,
he came across a running stream and decided
to walk along beside it.

As the dog walked along he looked down at
the water, then stopped in surprise. There was
another dog with a piece of meat in the water!
The dog had no idea it was his own reflection. His
only thought was that he had to have the other
piece of meat too. So he made a snap at the

The Boy who Cried Wolf

and other Aesop's Fables

Compiled by Vic Parker

First published in 2013 by Miles Kelly Publishing Ltd
Harding's Barn, Bardfield End Green, Thaxted, Essex, CM6 3PX, UK

Copyright © Miles Kelly Publishing Ltd 2013

2 4 6 8 10 9 7 5 3 1

Publishing Director Belinda Gallagher
Creative Director Jo Cowan
Editorial Director Rosie McGuire
Designer Joe Jones
Production Manager Elizabeth Collins
Reprographics Stephan Davis, Jennifer Hunt, Thom Allaway

ISBN 978-1-84810-933-9

Printed in China

British Library Cataloguing-in-Publication Data
A catalogue record for this book is available from the British Library

ACKNOWLEDGMENTS
The publishers would like to thank the following artists who have contributed to this book:
Cover: Frank Endersby
Advocate Art: Natalie Hinrichsen, Tamsin Hinrichsen
The Bright Agency: Marcin Piwowarski
Frank Endersby
Marco Furlotti
Jan Lewis (decorative frames)

Made with paper from a sustainable forest

www.mileskelly.net info@mileskelly.net

www.factsforprojects.com

dog in the water, but as he opened his mouth
he dropped the meat. It plopped into the brook
and was swirled away downriver.

It is very foolish to be greedy.

The Man
and the
Serpent

There was once a farmer who had a little boy, who was the joy of his life. The child was playing in the fields one day when by accident he stepped on a serpent's tail. The angry creature turned and bit the boy.

Within hours, he grew very ill, and the next day he died.

The farmer was filled with anger and grief. He grabbed his axe and went out into the fields, determined to find the serpent no matter how long it took. After much searching, he found its lair and waited outside. As soon as the serpent came out, the farmer swung at it with his axe. The serpent was too quick for the farmer to kill it, but he managed to cut off a part of its tail.

Of course the serpent was now furious too. To get its own back, it began biting the farmer's cattle, which all died just as the little boy had. When the farmer began losing his herd, he realized his anger had got the better of him. As much as he didn't want to, he realized that he would have to make up with the serpent.

The farmer took some food and honey to the

mouth of the serpent's lair and said, "Let's forgive and forget. Perhaps you were right to punish my son and take vengeance on my cattle, but I thought I was right in trying to revenge my child. Now that we are both satisfied, why can't we be friends?"

But the serpent flicked out its tongue and turned to slither away. "No, no," it said, "take your gifts away. You will never forget the death of your son, nor I the loss of my tail."

Injuries may be forgiven, but not forgotten.

The
Grasshopper
and the Ants

It was proving to be a long, hard winter and all the animals were suffering from the cold, the damp and the lack of food.

There was one particularly long spell of rain that seemed to go on for days on end. Then at last the sun came out one day and brightened up the winter bleakness. As the hot rays warmed the ground, the wet earth steamed and sent up clouds of mist. Some ants came out from their mound, bringing their store of corn, grain by grain. It had got rather damp so they decided

to lay it out in the sun to dry.

As the ants were hard at work fetching and carrying, along came a grasshopper who begged them to spare him a few grains, "For," he said, "I'm simply starving."

The ants stopped work for a moment, though this was against their instincts. "May we ask," they said, "what you were doing with yourself all last summer? Why didn't you collect a store of food for the winter?"

"The fact is," replied the grasshopper, "I was so busy singing that I didn't have the time."

"If you spent the summer singing," replied the ants, "you can't do better than spend the

winter dancing." And they chuckled and went on with their work.

It is best to be prepared in case hard times arrive.

The Donkey
and the
Lapdog

One day, a farmer went to his stables to check on his animals – among them his favorite donkey.

The farmer's lapdog went with him, and it danced about and licked its master's hand, as happy as could be. The farmer felt in his pocket, gave the lapdog a small snack, and sat down while he gave orders to his sons. The lapdog jumped onto its master's lap and lay there blinking while the farmer stroked its ears.

Upon seeing this, the donkey was filled with

jealousy, and wanted to be stroked and petted by the farmer too. So with a great pull, it broke loose from its halter and began prancing about just like the lapdog. At this sight, the farmer began laughing so hard that his sides ached.

The donkey thought that if the farmer was enjoying these antics so much, it must be doing a good job. So it went up to him, put its feet on his shoulders and tried to climb onto its master's lap.

When the farmer's sons saw the donkey squashing their father they rushed over with sticks and pitchforks. The donkey soon realized that fooling around so much that it hurt someone was not funny at all.

 Clumsy jesting is no joke.

The Lion in Love

There was once a mighty lion who happened to fall in love with a beautiful maiden. So the King of the Beasts went to the girl's parents to ask for her hand in marriage.

The parents were stunned – this was not what they had expected. They did not wish to give their daughter to the lion, yet they did not wish to enrage the King of the Beasts either.

At last the father said, "We feel privileged by Your Majesty's proposal, but our daughter is only a girl, and we fear that you might injure her by accident. May we suggest that you have your claws removed and your teeth pulled out. Then we will consider your proposal again."

The lion was downhearted at first. But he was so much in love that he did indeed have his claws trimmed and his big teeth taken out.

Then the lion went again to see the parents of his beloved, with high hopes that this time they would agree to let her marry him. But of course, this time they just laughed in his face, for now they had no reason to be afraid of him.

Love can tame the wildest.

The
Boy who
Cried Wolf

There was once a shepherd boy who tended his sheep at the foot of a mountain near a dark forest. He was out on the slopes all day by himself, and he often got lonely and bored.

One day, the shepherd boy thought up a plan whereby he could get a little company and some excitement. He left his flock unattended and rushed down the slopes towards his village. He pretended to be in a terrible panic and shouted, "Wolf! Wolf!" at the top of his voice.

The villagers came running to check that he was unharmed. When they realized there was no wolf, they returned grumbling, telling the boy not to shout at false alarms.

A few days later the naughty boy tried the same trick again. He ran down the mountainside screaming, "Wolf! Wolf!" And again the villagers came rushing to help him. This time they were angry to find there

was no wolf, just like the first time.

Just a few days later, the shepherd boy was watching his flocks as usual when a wolf really did come out of the forest and begin prowling around the sheep. Of course the boy set off down the mountainside crying, "Wolf! Wolf!"

even louder and in more of a panic than before.

But this time the villagers, who had already been fooled twice, thought the boy was again deceiving them. Nobody stirred to come to his aid. And so the wolf made a good meal of the boy's flock.

A liar will not be believed, even when he speaks the truth.

The Donkey
in the
Lion's Skin

Once upon a time, some hunters caught and killed a lion. They skinned the mighty beast and left its hide out in the sun to dry while they set off on another hunt. While the hunters were away, a donkey came wandering by. He was delighted to find the lion's skin and thought he would try it on. He put it over his head and shoulders and was sure that he looked good.

The donkey decided that finders were keepers, and he set off for home, draped in the hide. As he approached the village, everyone thought that a lion was approaching. People and animals fled as the donkey plodded closer.

The donkey realized what was happening, and was delighted. He lifted up his head with pride and brayed aloud. But that was a mistake — everyone realized who he was. Before he knew it, the villagers were pelting him with rotten vegetables for the trouble he had caused.

Fine clothes may disguise, but silly words will reveal a fool.

The FOX
and the
Goat

Once upon a time, an unfortunate fox fell into an unused well. The sides were steep and the well was too deep for him to climb out of. The fox was left helpless at the bottom, although thankful that the water had dried up.

At first the fox shouted for help, but nobody came, and after a while his voice grew tired. So he sat patiently, waiting for help to arrive, talking to himself from time to time.

Eventually a goat came past the well and heard the voice coming up from its depths.

Curious, he peered over and saw the fox, and asked what he was doing down there. "Oh, have you not heard?" replied the fox. "There is going to be a great drought, so I jumped down here to find some water in this old well.

Why don't you come down as well?"

The goat considered the fox's words and decided that they made good sense, so he jumped down into the well too. However, the fox immediately jumped on the goat's back and, by putting his paws on her horns, managed to jump up to the top of the well.

"Goodbye, friend," called the fox, trotting off to freedom and leaving the goat trapped below.

Never trust the advice of a person in difficulties.

The Donkey, the Rooster and the Lion

Once upon a time, a donkey and a rooster were in a farmyard together when a lion came prowling by. He had not eaten for days and was ravenous, so had set his sights upon the donkey first, as a more satisfying meal. The lion was just about to pounce when the rooster crowed at the top of its voice, "Cockadoodledoo!"

It is said that the one thing lions are afraid of is a rooster's crow, and this lion certainly fled as fast as he could. The donkey decided that the

lion must be very
cowardly indeed, and
galloped after him to
attack him himself.
However the lion heard the
donkey galloping behind him – and of
course he wasn't frightened of a
donkey at all. So he turned and
pounced, tearing the donkey to bits.

False confidence often
leads into danger.

27

The Donkey
and its
Driver

There **was once a donkey** that was being driven by its owner along the edge of a high cliff. A sudden noise in the undergrowth scared the donkey, which bolted. Unfortunately, it charged towards the clifftop – and in its fright, it didn't think to stop.

The owner was horrified and chased after the donkey, throwing himself at the beast to stop it going over the edge. The man managed to catch hold of the donkey's tail, and held on for dear life. However, the donkey kept trying so

hard to plunge over the cliff that in the end the man was forced to let it go, rather than be pulled over with it.

Don't be too stubborn in wanting your own way.

Jupiter
and the
Tortoise

Long ago in the early days of the world, the great god Jupiter ruled the Earth. The time came when he was to marry, and he was determined to hold a splendid wedding feast. Jupiter invited not just the other gods and goddesses but all the animals too. Every creature was delighted to be asked.

The wedding day arrived, the ceremony was performed, and then everyone gathered for the banquet. Jupiter looked around with pride, but he noticed that one animal was missing – the

tortoise. The feast was a huge success, but Jupiter was disappointed that the tortoise had not turned up, so he went to ask him why.

"I don't care for going out," said the tortoise, "there's no place like home."

Jupiter was enraged by this reply, and declared that from then onward the tortoise should carry his house on his back, and never be able to get away from home even if he wished to.

Be carfeful what you say, people might take you at your word.

The Farmer
and the
Fox

There was once a farmer who was bothered by a fox, which came prowling around his farmyard every night. Each morning, the farmer awoke to find yet more of his chickens, ducks or geese had been carried off.

So the farmer set a trap and caught the fox. As punishment, he tied a bunch of dry brushwood to the fox's tail and set fire to it.

The terrified creature ran off, trying to escape from the fire burning at its tail. However, the fox began making straight for the farmer's

fields, where the corn was standing ripe and ready for cutting. As the fox ran through the corn, it quickly caught fire, destroying the farmer's harvest.

Revenge is a double-edged sword.

The Two Frogs

There were once two frogs who were neighbors. One lived in a marsh, where there was plenty of water, which frogs love. The other dwelled in a lane some distance away, where there was no water except for the puddles which lay about after it had rained.

The marsh frog often worried about the other frog. She was anxious that if there were several weeks

without rain, the puddles would dry up – and so would her neighbor. The marsh frog warned her friend and pressed him to come and live with her in the marsh, for he would find his surroundings there far more comfortable and – more importantly – safe. But the other refused, saying that he could not bring himself to move from a place to which he had become accustomed.

A few days afterward it rained, and there were lots of puddles in the lane for the frog to splash in. Suddenly, a heavy wagon came down the lane, and the frog was crushed to death beneath the wheels.

Do not fear change, it is often for the better.

The Goatherder
and the
Goat

One day, a goatherder was out on a rocky mountainside where his goats had been grazing. It was time to round them up and take them down to the lowlands for the night. However, one of the goats had strayed off and was refusing to join the rest.

The goatherder tried to get her back by calling and whistling, but the goat took no notice of him. He grew more and more annoyed until at last he lost his temper completely, and picked up a stone and threw it at her. To his

horror, he saw that he had broken one of her horns.

The goatherder begged the goat not to tell his master, but she replied, "You silly boy, my broken horn will tell what's happened, even if I hold my tongue."

It's no use trying to hide what can't be hidden.

The
Astronomer

There was once an astronomer who enjoyed staying up at night and going out to watch the stars. The darker it was, the better it was for seeing the stars. So the man used to walk outside the town, away from all the lit lamps in the houses and streets, into the countryside where there was no light at all. Then he would make himself comfortable and spend hours watching the heavens.

One night, the astronomer had made his way into the fields and was walking along gazing